# THE PUPPY PLACE

## MIKI

# THE PUPPY PLACE

# MIKI

ELLEN
MILES

SCHOLASTIC INC.

ISBN 978-1-338-57220-9

10 9 8 7 6 5 4 3 2 1    20 21 22 23 24

Printed in the U.S.A.    40
First printing 2020

# CHAPTER ONE

"Did I hear the timer?" Ms. Holly cupped a hand to her ear. "I think Team Yummy's cupcakes might be done. Let's check!"

Charles jumped up to follow Ms. Holly to the oven. He and the rest of his team—Kendra, Alivia, and Luis—clustered around Ms. Holly as she pulled on an oven mitt, opened the door, slid out the rack, and poked a toothpick into one of the cupcakes. Charles's mouth watered as a sweet, chocolatey aroma wafted through the air. He could hardly wait for a taste.

Ms. Holly pulled out the toothpick and held it

up so everyone could see. "What do we think?" she asked.

"They're done!" said Alivia, jumping up and down. Charles could tell that she was eager to taste the cupcakes, too. But he also noticed that the toothpick was covered with brown goo.

Charles shook his head. "Not done," he said, remembering something Ms. Holly had mentioned earlier that day. "The toothpick has to come out clean."

"Very good, Charles," said Ms. Holly as she slid the rack back in and shut the oven door. "I see that you've been paying attention. We'll give them just three more minutes." She beamed at him, and Charles felt himself blushing. He didn't want to be a teacher's pet, but he liked it when Ms. Holly told him he'd done a good job.

Cooking lessons were so much fun. Charles was glad he had begged Mom to sign him up as soon as he saw the poster at the Littleton Community Center. He had been totally into cooking for a while now, and he wanted to learn more.

Today was Cupcake Day in cooking class. This was Charles's third lesson with Ms. Holly. She was the best teacher ever! She made everything so much fun, even when they were just learning about how to carry a knife when you were moving around the kitchen (point it downward, and don't run), how to clean up as you cooked (always keep your area tidy), or the correct way to wash your hands before you started any cooking at all (sing a whole verse of "Row, Row, Row Your Boat" while you scrub with soap and warm water).

Even though Charles was one of the youngest kids in class, Ms. Holly made him feel grown-up. She usually gave a few instructions at the beginning of each lesson, and then the teams were on their own. Ms. Holly was always reminding them that it was okay to make mistakes, too. "It didn't turn out the way you expected?" she'd ask. "Well, what do you think you might do differently next time?"

On the first Saturday, they had learned how to make spaghetti and meatballs and a Caesar salad. On the second Saturday, they had made homemade pizza with all kinds of crazy toppings. (Charles's team had put grapes and baloney on theirs, which was unexpectedly delicious.) And this week, they were doing cupcakes.

Each week, Ms. Holly divided up the class into three teams, and every time the teams were different. Charles liked everyone in the class, but today's team was the best. Alivia was really creative, Kendra was funny, and for some reason Luis loved washing pots and pans, which was perfect since Charles definitely did not.

When Ms. Holly had told them that they could

make up any flavor combinations they wanted for their cupcakes, Kendra was the one who'd come up with the perfect idea. "Chocolate cupcakes with pink peppermint frosting," she'd said.

"And we could decorate the top with crushed-up peppermint candy," Charles had added. He'd seen something like that on the baking show he and Dad had been watching lately.

The best part of cooking class was the end when they got to eat everything they'd made—but not until after Ms. Holly had tasted all their creations and declared one team the winner for the day. So far, Charles had not been on a winning team, but he had a feeling that today might be it. He watched through the oven window, counting the seconds until it was time to check the cupcakes again.

"How's Buddy?" Ms. Holly asked as they waited.

"He's great!" said Charles. Ms. Holly always

asked about Buddy, Charles's sweet brown puppy. She'd learned about him on the first day of class when they had played a "getting to know you" game. Charles had told everyone how his family fostered puppies, taking care of dogs who needed their help just until they could find each one the perfect forever home. It was never easy to give up the puppies when the time came, and with Buddy it had been pretty much impossible. The whole family had fallen in love with him. Buddy, Charles had told the class, was the only puppy the Petersons had ever decided to keep.

"Awww," Ms. Holly said when Charles talked about how cute Buddy was, with his soft brown fur and the white spot on his chest that was shaped like a heart. "I love dogs, but I'm allergic. You're so lucky."

Charles knew he was lucky. Being a foster family

was the best thing that had ever happened, and getting to keep Buddy was the icing on the cake.

Like . . . *peppermint* icing! Kendra had mixed up a bowlful of the stuff while they waited for their cupcakes to finish baking. Now, Charles poked a clean spoon into the bowl so he could taste the beautiful pink frosting. The flavor was sparkly and sweet. "Wow!" he said. "It's delicious!"

When the cupcakes were finally done, Ms. Holly helped pull them out of the oven. Charles and Luis popped them out of the tins and set them on a rack to cool. After a few minutes, Alivia spread a thick layer of pink frosting on each one. Then Kendra sprinkled flakes of crushed peppermint candy over the tops—and their creation was ready, just in time for the judging. They cleaned up their workstation while Ms. Holly walked around the room, looking over the finished cupcakes.

When she tasted Team Yummy's entry, Ms. Holly closed her eyes and pretended to faint. "Whoa," she said. "You guys really outdid yourselves. The flavor combination, the beautiful pink look, the candy sprinkles, the whole concept. It's a home run. Today's winner is definitely Team Yummy."

Charles and his teammates jumped up and down, giving each other high fives. "Yes!" yelled Luis. "Team Yummy rules!"

Charles knew their cupcakes were the best, but he tasted all the other teams' cupcakes, just to be sure. The rainbow ones that Team Scrumptious made looked really cool, but the flavor wasn't very exciting. He liked the butterscotch frosting on Team Tasty's cupcakes, but it didn't exactly go with the strawberry-flavored cake part. He had to agree with Ms. Holly. It was Team Yummy for the win.

Charles was buzzing as he ran out to meet Mom, who had come to pick him up. Ms. Holly followed the class outside to make sure everyone had a ride home. She waved at some other moms and called out a greeting to one of the dads. Then she peered into the Petersons' van. "Wait a minute," she said. "That's not Buddy."

# CHAPTER TWO

Charles frowned. Not Buddy? What did Ms. Holly mean? Of course it was Buddy. The little brown pup loved to ride along when Mom or Dad was picking someone up or just out doing errands. Charles ran to the van and tugged at the sliding door.

"Hold on there, cowboy," Mom called out the window. "The door is locked. I don't want Miki to escape."

"Miki?" Now Charles was really confused. Who was Miki? He stood on his tiptoes, cupped his hands around his face, and peered into the van's rear window. There, sitting in Buddy's usual spot in the backseat, was something small, white, and fluffy. It looked like a stuffie, the kind of stuffed animals (mostly dogs) that Lizzie collected. Then the fluffy thing twitched its ears, turned its head, and sniffed at the air for a moment, just long enough for Charles to become convinced. It wasn't a stuffie. It was a real, live puppy.

Charles ran around to the driver's side of the van and knocked on his mom's window. "Who is Miki?" he demanded. "Where did she come from? Are we fostering her? Can I get in and hold her?"

Mom put her window down and reached out to pat Charles's shoulder. "I'll tell you all about it on the way home," she said. "Let me grab Miki's leash before you get in."

"Maybe I could hold her, just for a minute?" asked Ms. Holly, who was still looking into the van. "I'm allergic to dogs. They make me sneeze, and my eyes itch like crazy. But she's so cute! It's worth it just this once."

Mom laughed. "She is pretty adorable," she admitted. "But I have a feeling she's going to be a bit of a handful."

"So we *are* fostering her!" yelled Charles. He started to jump up and down. Other kids who hadn't gotten into their parents' cars yet ran over and started to cluster around, trying to peek into the van's windows.

"What is it?" asked Kendra. "Is it a toy?"

"Wait, it's moving!" shouted Luis. "Maybe it's a robot."

"Everybody, please calm down," Mom said, from inside the van. She climbed into the backseat and clipped a leash onto the puppy's collar. Then she slid the back door open. "It's a real, live puppy, and if you want to meet her, you're going to have to use your indoor voices. And no sudden movements. We don't really even know this puppy, so let's be careful." She climbed out of the van, holding the little white puppy in her arms.

"Awwwwwww!" Everyone sighed at once.

"Is she for real?" shouted a girl named Kaitlynn. "I mean, she looks just like a little—"

"Shhhhh!" Alivia shushed her, finger over her lips. "Indoor voices, remember?"

Charles saw Mom and Ms. Holly smile at each other. Then Ms. Holly reached out her arms. "Can I?" she whispered. "Just for a second?"

Mom handed over the puppy. Charles watched as the fluffy puppy nestled herself into Ms. Holly's arms. Charles had been around a lot of puppies, but there was no question: This had to be the cutest puppy he had ever seen. She had floppy little ears and an adorable tiny black nose. Her eyes were black and shiny, and her tongue, when she stuck it out to lick Ms. Holly's face, was as pink as an apple blossom in springtime. Her coat looked so soft and fluffy, like the part of a dandelion that you blow into the wind for good luck.

"Her name is Miki," Mom said. "Her owners had to give her up because they're moving across the country, to an apartment building that doesn't allow dogs." She put a hand on Charles's shoulder. "I just picked Miki up from your aunt Amanda's doggy day care. She's a regular there. Amanda says the owners are completely heartbroken. She promised them that we would take good care of Miki and find her a very special home."

"Such a cute name for such a cute dog," said Ms. Holly. She buried her nose in the dog's neck. Charles waited for her to start sneezing, but she just closed her eyes and took in a long, deep breath. "Ahhh, that puppy smell," she said. "Even better than chocolate cupcakes." Then she opened her eyes. "Okay, I better give her back before my allergies kick in." She handed the little pup back to Mom.

"Her owners told Amanda that the name Miki means 'beautiful' in Japanese," Mom said. She held Miki carefully as she looked around at the crowd that had gathered. "Okay, kiddos, you can each have a moment with her. Just give Miki a gentle pat. And remember to move slowly and carefully so you don't scare her."

One by one, each of the kids went up to Miki and touched her gently. Kendra almost looked like she was going to cry. "I just can't believe how cute she is," she said, after she'd had her turn. She squeezed her hands together and sighed. "I've never seen a real, live dog who looked like that."

"I'm going to ask my mom if we can have another dog," said Alivia. "We only have three. And this one is really small. The other dogs would all love her."

"What kind of dog is she?" asked one of the moms, who had also gotten in line to take a turn petting Miki.

"She is a bichon frise, according to her owners," said Charles's mom. She pronounced it like "bishun freeze." "Kind of a fancy breed. Very expensive to buy, from what I understand."

Charles hated to think about people buying and selling dogs when there were so many dogs out there who needed homes.

"She's quite calm," said Ms. Holly. "Not like some little dogs, the kind that are always running around and yapping."

"I think that's because she was playing all day with all the other dogs at doggy day care," Mom told her. "Amanda says she's usually a real live wire. She loves attention and can't get enough. I guess her owners taught her all kinds of tricks."

"Like what?" Charles asked.

Mom shrugged. "I didn't have a chance to ask," she said. "I suppose we'll find out soon enough."

Miki began to wriggle in Mom's arms, struggling to get down. "Okay, okay," said Mom. She bent over and set Miki on the pavement. The little dog shook herself all over so that her fluffy white fur stood out. She looked around at the crowd surrounding her, cocking her head.

*You want to see a trick? I'll show you a trick!*

Then she stood up on her hind legs and began to prance around in a circle, holding her tiny paws in front of her. Everybody gasped and began to cheer. Miki's black eyes sparkled with the fun of it all as she danced, spinning around and around.

# CHAPTER THREE

Charles rode home holding Miki on his lap. She was light as a feather, and so warm and soft. He couldn't stop kissing the top of her fluffy head. "She's amazing, Mom," he said. "Did you ever see a dog dance like that before, up on her hind legs?"

Mom shook her head, smiling into the rearview mirror. "She's special, all right," she said. "And I think she knows it, too. She's used to getting a lot of attention, according to Amanda."

"Well, she deserves it," said Charles, nuzzling the little dog. "Don't you love the way her hair puffs out all around her head?"

"That's because she's been getting very fancy

grooming, at Isabella's—you know, that expensive pet salon?" Mom said. "That's the kind of thing that worries me. Amanda promised me that this pup isn't spoiled, but it's pretty obvious that she has been pampered."

Charles had a feeling Mom was remembering Princess, a very cute Yorkie puppy the Petersons had once fostered. Princess had been very, very spoiled, and she had not been easy to take care of. Not only did she eat special food, but she had her own special dishes. Charles laughed. "You're thinking of Princess, aren't you? I don't think Miki's like that," he said. "She can't help it that she's so adorable, or that she knows tricks, or that she's had fancy haircuts." He already felt protective of Miki. "It's not like her owners gave us a long list about her care, like Princess's did."

Mom nodded. "That's true," she said. "I'll keep an open mind. Let's start by seeing how she gets along with other dogs." She pulled into the Petersons' driveway. "Take her out in the backyard, and I'll let Buddy out to meet her."

Charles got out of the van, holding Miki carefully. She was so tiny! He was afraid he might hurt her. But the second he put her down on the lawn in the Petersons' fenced backyard, she began to tear around just like any other puppy. She was longer than she was tall, but her short little legs were amazingly fast. In a second she'd dashed past the swing set, around the rosebushes, and back to Charles. She spun around on her hind legs for a moment, grinning at him, then raced off for another lap around the yard, like a fluffy little white rocket.

Charles heard laughter and turned to see Lizzie at the back door. "They call that the bichon blitz," she said. "I've heard about it, but I've never seen it."

Charles blinked. How did Lizzie do it? She'd seen the puppy for two seconds, and not only did she already guess Miki's breed, she even knew some weird fact about bichon frise dogs. His sister was like a walking encyclopedia of dog information.

"Let's see what Buddy thinks," Lizzie said, stepping aside to let the little brown puppy out. Buddy walked to the top of the porch stairs and paused there for a moment, watching Miki tear around the yard. Then he flew down the stairs to join her. Buddy loved to chase and be chased, the faster the better.

"She's so cute!" Lizzie said. "When Mom told me she was bringing home a fluffy little puppy, I wondered if she'd be spoiled rotten. But Miki acts just like a regular dog."

"Well, not exactly," said Charles. "Wait till you see what she can do." He waited until the next time Miki paused nearby. "Miki, dance for us," he said, waving his hand. He didn't know if the command and hand signal would work, but Miki seemed to understand what he wanted. Right away she stood up on her hind legs and spun around in circles. Her tiny pink tongue stuck out as she panted, and her eyes were bright.

Lizzie laughed and clapped her hands. "That's right! Now I remember something else about this breed," she said. "I think they're from Italy, and they used to work with street performers. Doing something just like that, maybe. Dancing while somebody sang or played music."

Miki finished her dancing and grinned up at Charles and Lizzie with her head tilted at the most adorable angle possible. Her tiny tail wagged as fast as a hummingbird's wings.

*What should I do next?*

"Let's see what other tricks she knows," said Lizzie. "Miki, sit."

Miki sat.

She gazed up at Lizzie, her head tilted.

*Um, that was kinda easy. How about asking me to do something a little more challenging?*

"Shake, Miki," said Charles. Miki reached out one tiny paw and rested it for just a second on Charles's outstretched hand. Then she sat up on her haunches and held up a paw for a high five, without even being asked. After that she offered the other paw, then went for low fives with each paw. Charles and Lizzie cracked up.

"She's, like, three steps ahead of us," said Lizzie.

"She's amazing," said Charles. "She's like a superstar."

Buddy sat watching. When Charles looked at

him, he held up his paw, looking at Charles with a wistful expression.

"Aw, Buddy," said Charles, shaking his puppy's paw. "Don't be jealous. You're smart, too! You know lots of tricks."

Charles and Lizzie spent the rest of the afternoon in the backyard, playing with the puppies. Buddy got tired after a while and went to lie down by the back door, but Miki just kept going and going. If Charles and Lizzie talked about something else for a moment, she reminded them with another trick.

*How about this? Or this!? See what I can do?*

She sat up pretty. She rolled over. She chased her tail one way and then chased it the other way. She did her dance again and again, spinning around in circles while her fluffy white fur spun out, too. Miki jumped up into Charles's arms when he held them out, and she leapt through a hoop that Lizzie made with her arms.

"She reminds me of Sweetie," said Lizzie after one of Miki's jumps.

"I know," said Charles, thinking of the sweet little miniature poodle their family had once fostered. Sweetie had also been really good at tricks, and Charles and his friends had made her the star of a circus they put on for friends and family. Sweetie was a charmer, and the Petersons had found her the perfect forever home. Charles was sure they could do the same for Miki.

# CHAPTER FOUR

The next morning, Charles lingered at home until the very last minute, hating to leave Miki for even a few hours. Why did he have to go to school? Miki was so much fun to be around. Charles had never met a puppy with such a sparkling, merry personality. Miki seemed to be in a great mood all the time. She bounced around happily, never missing an opportunity for more attention.

"Like last night," Charles told his best friend, Sammy, during recess. They were waiting for their turn at the plate during a kickball game. "After dinner Buddy curled up on his bed. But Miki still wanted to show off her tricks. She kept it up until we were all yawning and couldn't stay up a minute longer."

"She should be on that show *America's Most Talented Pets*," Sammy said. "I mean, if everything you're saying is true, she could probably win the top prize. You know, just ten thousand dollars," he added, shrugging. He acted like it was no big deal.

"Ten thousand dollars!" Charles had seen the show, of course. It seemed like the winning pets usually had a whole act that they did, along with their owners. He'd forgotten that the top prize was so big.

Charles was distracted for the rest of the day at school, picturing himself and Miki on a stage lit with whirling laser lights—the music pounding as he and Miki did their act. He imagined a panel of judges watching in amazement as Miki charmed them, and he pictured the audience going wild with cheers and applause. He wasn't exactly sure what he was doing up there, but otherwise he could see the whole thing, including the part where the top judge shook Charles's and Miki's hands and gave them a giant check for Ten! Thousand! Dollars!

Then Charles could announce that Miki needed a forever home, and the Petersons would be flooded with calls and texts from people who wanted to adopt her. This was the point in the daydream where Charles pictured Mom and Dad agreeing that Buddy needed an adorable little sister, and that Miki could stay with them forever. As long as he was dreaming, why not go all the way and make it so Miki became part of the Peterson family?

After school, Sammy and Charles practically sprinted all the way home. Miki and Buddy met them at the front door, all grins and wagging tails. "Wow, she really is cute," said Sammy, dropping to his knees to pet Miki. He petted Buddy, too. "And so are you," he said. Sammy loved Buddy and didn't want him to be jealous.

"She was a good girl today," Mom reported. "She ran through her tricks for me, but then she settled down and took it easy. She and Buddy napped for most of the afternoon while I worked, so I'm sure they're both ready for some playtime."

Charles and Sammy took the puppies into the backyard. Sammy hooted with laughter when he saw how Miki tore around the yard.

"It's the bichon blitz," Charles told him. Once she had worked out her energy a little by running around, Charles called Miki over. "Sit, Miki," he said.

Miki's butt hit the ground before he'd even

finished the command. She smiled up at him, tilted her head at that adorable angle, and wagged her little tail.

*Easy-peasy. What's next?*

"Shake," Charles said, holding out his hand.

Miki put her paw in his hand. Then, without him asking, she offered her other paw. Then she got up on her hind legs and offered him a high five, then a low five with each paw.

*Come on, let's make this fun!*

Sammy burst out laughing. "Wow, you weren't kidding. She is a superstar. What else can she do?"

"She likes to dance," Charles said, and before the words were out of his mouth Miki was up on her hind legs, spinning around. She grinned up at the boys as she whirled.

*Like this, you mean? I do like it. I mean, I love it! I love to dance.*

"She's amazing!" Sammy said. "That's it! We have to put together an act for *America's Most Talented Pets*. She can dance while we sing." He jumped up and started waving his arms around.

"Um," said Charles. He was glad Sammy was so enthusiastic, but he couldn't quite picture it. "Wouldn't we need a little more than just the two of us up there singing?" Charles once had very bad stage fright, but he'd mostly gotten over it when he acted in a community theater play. He could picture himself onstage, but not just standing there with one other boy, singing. On TV. In front of millions of people. Was Sammy really serious? Charles had thought they were just fooling around.

"Sure, of course we'd have more," said Sammy. "You could play keyboards, right? And I can play drums."

Charles raised his eyebrows. It was true that he'd taken a few piano lessons, and he did have a keyboard in the garage. But it was more of a toy than a real instrument. It had built-in loops so it sounded like you were really making music when you touched just about any key. And the only drums Sammy had were a pair of bongos his grandpa had given him. His mom had made him keep them in the basement since she couldn't stand the racket Sammy made when he banged away on them.

"And Lizzie can play tambourine!" Sammy was so excited his words were tripping over each other. "We can have a whole band. We already know a bunch of songs." He began to sing one of the songs their class had performed at the school's last open house.

Miki had been looking back and forth as they talked, as if she was following their conversation. Now she stood up on her hind legs and began to dance in rhythm to Sammy's singing.

*We can do this thing! I'm so ready.*

Charles cracked up. Maybe Sammy was right: Miki was born to perform. "Okay," he said, shrugging. "I guess we're gonna go for it."

# CHAPTER FIVE

Charles and Sammy headed for the garage, bringing Miki and Buddy along. "Hmm," said Charles, when he turned on the lights and spotted his keyboard in a corner behind a tangle of bicycles, lawn tools, and yard games. "I don't know if . . ."

"Come on," said Sammy. "We can clear out that corner in no time." He waded in through a maze of snow tires and cross-country skis that had never exactly been put away for the summer.

Charles gulped. Now he understood why his dad kept talking about how they really had to clean out the garage. This was not what he'd had in mind for the afternoon. But Sammy was already moving things around, with Miki and Buddy "helping" by finding old tennis balls and baseball mitts. Charles took a breath and followed them into the mess.

A half hour later, they'd cleared enough room for a practice space. Charles's keyboard stood in the middle, and Sammy had run home to grab his bongos. By now, Buddy had curled up for a nap, but Miki was still prancing around, investigating her new surroundings.

"What should we play first?" Sammy asked.

Charles tried to remember how the keyboard worked. He pushed a button and hit a few keys. A repeating beat that sounded like elevator music started up.

Sammy grinned. "Sounds great!" he said. He began to bang on the bongos, nodding along.

Miki stood on her hind legs in front of the keyboards and began to spin around. Her ears flew out and her eyes sparkled as she danced.

*Oh, yeah. I love music!*

"Look at her go!" crowed Sammy. "I told you! She's a natural celebrity."

Charles grinned at him and kept playing. He knew they were just fooling around, but it was a lot of fun. Especially with Miki dancing along.

"Woo-hoo!" someone called out.

Charles's hands froze on the keys. He looked up to see Lizzie standing by the door with her hands on her hips. "What are you guys doing in here? You're making a racket, but Miki's dancing is amazing."

The whole story spilled out, with Sammy and Charles taking turns to explain their plan for getting on *America's Most Talented Pets*. Miki stopped dancing when the music ended, and pranced over to Lizzie for some pets.

"And you can be in the band, too," Sammy said. "The judges will love an all-kid band."

Lizzie laughed. "Sure, they will," she said. Then she picked up the tambourine Charles had found under a big flowerpot, and began to bang it on her hip.

Charles hit another button on his keyboard, and it made a noise like a trumpet.

"Great!" Lizzie said. She started to bounce around as she banged the tambourine. Miki ran in circles around her, then started to do a whole new dance step where she hopped forward and backward.

They all cracked up. It was hard to keep playing and singing when Miki was being so funny and cute. "Maybe Laureen knows someone who would be interested in adopting Miki," Lizzie said. Laureen was a woman who danced with her dogs. They had met when Lizzie was taking care of a beautiful Irish setter named Rusty.

They played for a long time, just fooling around

with their instruments. No matter how silly the music got, Miki danced gracefully, sometimes on her hind legs and sometimes on all four paws, but always with a big happy doggy grin. Charles could tell she was having the time of her life.

"Bravo!" someone called, when they'd finished. It was Mom, carrying the Bean on her hip. She clapped when they stopped playing, and the Bean clapped, too. "You guys sure are having a good time. What made you pull out your instruments?"

Charles explained about *America's Most Talented Pets.* "And we can win ten thousand dollars," he said. "And get famous and everything. And find Miki a really great home, of course." He knew that Mom was always eager to find homes for their foster pups.

Mom raised her eyebrows. "Well, maybe. Anyway, you're having fun, and so is Miki."

"Fun!" yelled the Bean, struggling to get down.

"You want to make music with the big kids?" Mom asked. She set the Bean down and he toddled toward Charles.

"I play!" the Bean said, reaching up for the keyboard.

"Mom," Charles pleaded. "Can't he play something else? This is my instrument."

"No, my insto—instam—MINE!" yelled the Bean.

Charles rolled his eyes. He picked his brother up and let him push some keys while Lizzie and Sammy banged away on the drums and tambourine. The truth was, it didn't sound so much worse when a tiny kid was playing.

Miki sure couldn't tell the difference. She spun and hopped, dancing happily. The Bean laughed his googly laugh as he poked at the keys, bouncing up and down in Charles's arms.

Mom gave Charles a grateful look. "Dinner's

almost ready," she said, "so it's time to finish up for today."

Later that night, after dinner, Mom pulled out her laptop and the whole family sat down together to check out an old episode of *America's Most Talented Pets*. The show was amazing! There was a parrot who could quote Shakespeare, a cat who knew how to fetch, and a beagle who sang the national anthem. "Miki is as good as any of them, isn't she?" Charles said. He knew their band wasn't really ready for prime time, but it was fun to dream. And Miki really was very talented.

Mom scrolled through the website. "Here! It tells how to apply to be on the show." She clicked on the link and read silently for a moment. Then she sighed. "Oh, well," she said.

# CHAPTER SIX

"What?" Charles asked. He had a sinking feeling in his stomach. That sigh of Mom's did not make it sound like good news.

"*America's Most Talented Pets* is now booking acts for next year's season," Mom read. "Please submit your video now for consideration. We will call within six months with our decision." She closed her laptop and sat back. "Next year's season," she said. "That's way too far off. Miki needs to be in her forever home long before that."

"Noooo!" said Lizzie.

"Oh, too bad," said Dad. "I was totally picturing Miki on that show."

"Bad, bad, bad," echoed the Bean.

"Sammy's going to be bummed," said Charles. Unlike his friend, he had never really believed that they could win ten thousand dollars, but it had been fun to think about. He dragged himself to bed soon after that, feeling pretty bummed himself.

"I'm sure you'll come up with another good idea," Mom called as he trudged up the stairs with Miki at his heels.

The next morning, Charles woke to Miki licking his face.

*Come on, wake up! Time to practice some more. That was so much fun.*

Charles groaned. "Hi, Miki," he said. "I hate to tell you this, but I can't hang out today. Today is my last cooking class." He threw back the covers, sat up, and gathered the little fluffball into his arms. "I'll miss you!" he whispered as he nuzzled her fluffy, soft fur. Miki was so cute. He couldn't believe she wasn't going to get to be on TV—at least not while he was fostering her.

Today's class, which was three hours instead of two, was going to be a special one. Charles was sure that Mom knew something about it, but she wouldn't tell him, no matter how many times he asked.

When Charles arrived at the community center, he found Ms. Holly alone in the kitchen. "Oops, I guess I'm early," he said.

"That's cool," said Ms. Holly. "We'll have time for you to tell me how that adorable Miki is doing."

Charles filled Ms. Holly in while she bustled around, getting ready for class.

"Aw, that's a shame," she said, when she heard about how long it would take to get on *America's*

*Most Talented Pets.* "It sounded like a great idea. Maybe you can still do something with your new band, though."

"Like what?" Charles asked.

"Do you know what a busker is?" Ms. Holly asked as she laid out knives, bowls, measuring cups and spoons, casserole pans, and baking sheets.

Charles shook his head. "Nope."

"It's a person who makes music or does an act on the street for people walking by. Usually they set out a hat or a basket for people to put money in if they like the act." She smiled. "My husband was a busker on the streets of Brooklyn when I first met him. I think I fell in love at first sight when I saw him juggling watermelons."

Charles laughed. He liked the idea of busking. With Miki dancing in front of them, they'd be sure to get a lot of attention, even if their band wasn't exactly professional. They'd have a good time, and if they actually made any money, they could donate it to Caring Paws, the local animal shelter. "Thanks for the idea," he told Ms. Holly as the rest of the class began to trickle in. "That sounds like fun."

Soon everyone had arrived, and the room buzzed with excited talking. Ms. Holly clapped her hands. "Okay, kiddos. Listen up," she said. "Today's class is going to be a little different. We're going to be taking a field trip."

"Cool!"

"Where are we going?"

"Right now?"

Everybody started talking again. Ms. Holly crossed her arms and waited. Finally, the room grew quiet. She smiled. "We're going to one of my favorite places, the farmers market. Has anyone been there before?"

Charles raised his hand, along with some of the other kids. The farmers market took place in a little park in the middle of Littleton, under the shade of some big trees. There were always lots of canopy tents set up, under which the farmers displayed their colorful vegetables and flowers. Charles liked going to the market when the weather was good. There was always something interesting to see there, and sometimes Mom or Dad let him get a treat, like kettle corn or homemade chocolates. "I have," he said. "I love it!"

Ms. Holly nodded. "So do I," she said. "There's nothing better than buying food from the people who are growing it. Farmers are my heroes, and I love to support them. Plus, fresh, locally grown fruits and vegetables are extra-delicious. You'll see! We're going to shop for our ingredients there, then come back here and cook ourselves a fabulous lunch."

"How will we pay for all the ingredients?" Kendra asked.

"When you let me know how much money you need, I'll pay. It's part of the class," said Ms. Holly. She reached behind the table and pulled out three colorful woven baskets.

"Team Tomato," she called out. "Charles, Kendra, and Gordon. You'll be making our main dish, ratatouille."

"Like in the movie?" Charles asked. "But what is it, anyway?"

"Mmmm," said Ms. Holly as she handed his team a red-and-purple basket. "It's summer in a bowl, that's what! A luscious vegetable stew starring tomatoes, eggplants, garlic, onions, and a whole bunch of other beautiful veggies."

"Ew," said Luis, and a few other kids groaned.

Charles thought it sounded kind of interesting. He had been branching out with what vegetables he liked to eat, but he hadn't tried eggplant yet.

"Team Carrot," Ms. Holly said, calling out some names. "Our appetizer squad. You'll be cutting up fresh, raw vegetables and creating a delicious, herby dip." She handed an orange basket to a boy named Jerome.

"And last but not least, Team Apple." Ms. Holly handed over the last of the baskets, a red-and-green one. "You'll be baking our dessert—a scrumptious, bubbling, cinnamon-smelling apple crisp. With ice cream on top, of course."

Charles felt his mouth watering. This was going to be the best field trip ever!

# CHAPTER SEVEN

It was an easy walk to the farmers market. Charles smiled when he saw the colorful tents set up in two long lines across the grass. People strolled up and down, holding little kids by the hand or walking dogs on leashes. Dogs! There sure were a lot of them. Charles saw a chocolate Lab, a Boston terrier, and a greyhound in just the first few minutes. All the dogs seemed friendly and happy, and if their leashes got tangled together now and then as they sniffed and pawed at one another, their owners didn't seem to mind.

The market was a happy place, full of color. Buckets of bright flowers stood in one stall, next to a stall that displayed carrots in all colors of the rainbow. "We should add some of those to our recipe," Charles said, pointing to them.

"Maybe," said Gordon doubtfully.

"Ms. Holly said we should walk up and down and look at all the stalls before we buy anything," Kendra reminded them. "Anyway, look over there! Free samples of maple candy."

They zigged and zagged their way between the tents, along with the other teams. Ms. Holly seemed to be always nearby, keeping an eye on everyone and nodding when they pointed to things. "Those are wild mushrooms," she said, when Charles stopped to look at a pile of golden-yellow trumpets. "They're called chanterelles, and they are so yummy."

Charles didn't think he had ever tried wild mushrooms. He wanted to. He wanted to try everything. That was the way to become a good cook, or even a famous chef, Ms. Holly had told them. "Don't be timid," she said. "Taste everything, and taste it again. Some foods take a while to grow on you."

He and his teammates walked up and down the whole market, looking over everything that was for sale. "Cookies!" Kendra said in a Cookie Monster voice as they passed a stall selling giant chocolate-chip cookies. "Want cookies!" Gordon and Charles pulled her away, back to the vegetable stall they had liked best. The woman who ran it was really friendly and very interested in their cooking class project.

Charles picked out a shiny purple eggplant, and Kendra and Gordon added tomatoes, peppers, onions, and garlic. "Zucchini?" Kendra asked, and Charles nodded. She added it to the pile.

"Anything else?" asked the woman.

"Basil?" said Charles, remembering. She reached

over and picked up a bunch of the bright green herb, handing it over with a smile. Then she began adding up prices on her calculator as she placed the vegetables into their basket. Charles held his breath, hoping they hadn't spent too much.

Ms. Holly showed up just as the woman announced the total. "Perfect," said Ms. Holly, handing over some money. She and the woman seemed to know each other, and they chatted for a while about the weather.

"Enjoy your cooking," said the woman, finally. "And eating!"

Gordon set the basket down under a tree, and they wandered some more. As he was checking out a display of handmade coffee mugs, wondering if Mom might like one for Christmas, Charles felt something tickling his ankles. He looked down to see Miki's adorable face staring up at him as she put her tiny feet on his legs. She tugged at the leash Mom held, whining happily.

*My friend! I didn't know I was going to see you here. Happy, happy, happy!*

"Miki!" Charles said, kneeling down to pet and kiss her. Kendra, Gordon, and some of the other kids ran over, too. So did Ms. Holly, who knelt right down to pet Miki. Finally, Charles, looked up. "Hi, Mom," he remembered to say. "What are you doing here?"

"Same as you," she said, smiling. "Shopping!"

Within a few moments it seemed as if everyone at the market was clustered around to say hi to Miki. They cooed over her and petted her, and Charles could tell that she loved the attention. When Ms. Holly said it was time to head back to the kitchen, he gave Miki one more hug. "I'll see you soon, back at home," he told her.

As he and his teammates picked up their basket and left the farmers market, Charles turned back for one last look. He couldn't even see the little white pup, since she was still surrounded by people. She was like a magnet—and they hadn't even seen her dance yet. That's when the light bulb went off in Charles's brain. The farmers market was the perfect place for busking.

# CHAPTER EIGHT

"Where's Miki?" Charles asked, when he climbed into Mom's van later in the day.

"Hello to you, too," said Mom, smiling. "Don't worry. Miki is fine. She was having such a good time dancing while Lizzie sang—I couldn't stand to make her come with me to pick you up."

"They're still practicing?" Charles asked as he climbed into the backseat and buckled up. "Even though we can't get on TV?"

Mom nodded. "Lizzie has this big idea about performing with her, to raise money for Caring Paws. She'll tell you all about it."

"Busking!" said Charles, laughing. "That was going to be my idea."

"Where did you hear about busking?" Mom asked, looking at him in the rearview mirror.

"Ms. Holly told me," Charles said. "Her husband used to be a busker. And I figured out the best place for it: at the farmers market!"

Mom nodded. "Hmm," she said. "There are certainly a lot of people there, and they did seem to like Miki today. I have to admit I'm not crazy about you performing on the street, but I bet Dad will go along with you and keep an eye on things."

Then she made Charles tell her about his day since they'd seen each other at the market. "How did the ratatouille turn out?" she asked.

Charles gave her a full report on their lunch and how delicious it had been. "I think I really like eggplant," he reported. "The veggie dip was great, too. And of course the apple crisp was the best." He was going to miss Ms. Holly. Maybe he could take her advanced class next time she offered it.

When they got home, Charles heard music from the garage. Sammy was already there, playing the bongos while Lizzie sang and banged a tambourine. And between them was Miki, dancing on her hind legs. She tilted her head and gave Charles a doggy grin when he came in.

*What do you think? The act is really coming along—thanks to me!*

Charles swooped in to give Miki a hug. She was absolutely irresistible! Then he stood up and clapped his hands, applauding for the band. "Sounds great," he said, heading for his keyboard.

"Did Mom tell you?" asked Lizzie. "About how we're going to take the act on the road?"

Charles nodded. "I'm in," he said. "I always wanted to be a busker." He took a moment to enjoy the bewildered look on Lizzie's face. "A street performer," he explained. "And I have the perfect spot for us: the farmers market!"

Lizzie didn't always like it when somebody else had great ideas. She took a moment to think about it, then grinned at Charles. "You're right," she said. "The farmers market will be perfect."

Sammy had been thinking, too. "Maybe that should be our band's name," he said. "The Buskers."

Lizzie groaned. "We can do better than that," she said. "I was thinking we could be Lizzie and the Legends."

Charles raised his eyebrows. "Wait, why do you get to be the star? How about Charles and—" he thought for a second—"and the Champions?"

Sammy didn't look happy about that idea, and neither did Lizzie. Quickly, Charles changed course. "Miki's really the star," he said. "I mean, she's the reason for the whole thing. We only play so she can dance, right?"

They all nodded.

Miki let out a little yip and took a few dance steps.

*That's right, it's all about meeeeee!*

Charles thought for a moment, turning over ideas in his head. "So how about . . . Miki and the Melody Makers?" he said.

There was a moment of silence.

"It's good," said Lizzie, a little grudgingly.

"It's great," said Sammy. "I think we found our name."

Miki yipped again. She pranced over to Charles and put her paws up on his knees.

*It's perfect!*

"Now, can we get back to our rehearsal?" Lizzie asked. "What song is next?"

Charles punched a couple of buttons on his keyboard and a salsa beat filled the air.

Lizzie jumped right in, banging her tambourine. Sammy thumped on his bongos. Miki pranced and spun in the middle of the garage.

"I think Miki liked that one," said Sammy when they stopped.

"I think Miki loves to perform," said Lizzie. "It's in her genes. You can tell how much she loves attention. I wonder if she knows how to take a bow."

Instantly, Miki stretched out her front feet and

put her butt in the air, the pose that Buddy used whenever he wanted to play.

*Sure, I do!*

They all laughed. "That's great!" said Sammy. "We can have her do that at the end of our show. The crowd will love it."

"Crowd?" Charles had not exactly been picturing a crowd. More like people walking by and sort of listening for a while, on their way to buy vegetables for the week. He felt a familiar twist in his stomach, then reminded himself that he had learned to enjoy performing. Once, when he'd acted in that play, and another time when he was part of a piano recital. He could do this—he could! Especially with Miki there. All eyes would be on the beautiful dancing dog; he was sure of it.

# CHAPTER NINE

"I'll be right nearby if you need me," Dad said, after he'd helped Charles set up his keyboard under one of the biggest trees the following Saturday. "Have fun!"

The farmers market was in full swing, with lots of people roaming around carrying baskets full of flowers and vegetables. Miki's eyes were bright as she watched the action, and she wagged her tail when she saw a pair of poodles prance by. "Stay, Miki," said Charles. Lizzie had her on a leash just in case.

"Ready?" asked Sammy. "A one and a two and a three and a four," he counted out the beat.

Charles hit the wrong button and the notes came out all funny. His hands were sweaty and his heart was beating fast. "Wait," he said, fumbling with the settings on his keyboard. "Start over." It didn't really matter—nobody was watching yet.

Miki had already started to dance, and now she cocked her head at him, as if to ask what the problem was.

*Nothing to be nervous about! Watch me!*

"Take a breath," Lizzie whispered to Charles. "You've got this."

Charles took a deep breath in, and let it out slowly. He nodded. "Right. I've got this." He nodded to Sammy, and Sammy counted out the beat again. This time, Charles found the right rhythm. Lizzie joined in, banging her tambourine, and

Sammy, grinning, thumped on his bongos. Miki twirled and pranced in the middle, holding her little front paws in front of her chest.

"Ooooh, look at that cute little puppy!" A woman and her toddler daughter stopped to stare.

"She's adorable!" said another woman, who held three gigantic sunflowers in her hand.

"Look at that dog dance!" Soon a small crowd had gathered. Just as Charles had imagined, all eyes were on Miki. But he saw that people were tapping their feet and swaying to the music, so maybe it sounded okay. When they stopped playing, there was a burst of applause. Three people stepped forward to put money into the straw hat that Lizzie had placed upside down in front of Charles's keyboard, and several others stopped to read the sign Lizzie had made about Caring Paws and all the terrific animals they had for adoption. Miki was a great advertisement for how special a rescued dog could be, but Charles and his family had agreed that they wouldn't let just anyone adopt her. She was so special. Only the most perfect home would do for Miki.

"Take a bow, Miki," said Lizzie.

Miki went into a play bow with her little legs stretched way out in front. Her little tail wagged as she grinned at the crowd. People laughed and cheered and clapped. "More!" called someone in the back.

Charles smiled at Sammy and gave him a thumbs-up. Then he switched to a different beat for their next song. Busking was a whole lot of fun!

Dad came by at the end of that song and joined in the applause. "I can tell you're having a great time," he said to Charles. "And it looks like you've raised a few dollars for the shelter." He waved toward the straw hat, which was overflowing with bills and change. "Maybe you'll even find Miki a home!"

Charles felt his stomach knot up. The truth was, he didn't really want to find Miki just any old home. He knew that performing was in this puppy's blood, and that she wouldn't really be happy unless she could share her amazing talent.

But he just nodded at Dad. "Great," he said.

"Let me know when you're ready for a break and a snack," Dad said. "There's a girl over there selling some great-looking cupcakes."

Charles laughed and craned his neck to see where Dad was pointing. Sure enough, there was Kendra standing behind a long table full of baked goods. He waved to her and she waved back. "Maybe in a bit," he said. First, he wanted to play some more. He started up another beat and waited for the others to join in.

Miki's tail began to wag double time as she leapt

to her hind legs and began a joyous dance, bob-
bing to the rhythm of the drums and tambourine.

*I love this one!*

When they finished their last song a little later,
the crowd applauded and put more money into the
hat. Lizzie went off to buy kettle corn and lemon-
ade for everyone, and Sammy went to sit under a
tree. Charles kept noodling on his keyboard. He
still wasn't ready to stop. Miki danced along as
Charles played.

"Aha! So this is why I don't have much of an
audience today." Charles looked up from his keyboard to see a tall, lanky man dressed in bright
green pants, a yellow polka-dotted shirt, and red
suspenders. He wore a long-billed baseball cap
sideways on his head, his curly blond hair spilling
out from under it.

"Silly Billy!" Charles said. He recognized the man from birthday parties he'd been to. Silly Billy was hilarious. He made balloon animals, told jokes, played the ukulele, and juggled.

"That's me," said the man. "I'm, um, the official entertainment for the market today. But nobody's watching me. Everybody's talking about this cutie!" He gestured to Miki, who was sitting up pretty now, next to the keyboard. "I hear she's something else. No wonder everybody came over here to watch."

"Oops, sorry," said Charles. "We didn't know—"

"It's okay." Silly Billy waved a hand. "There's always room for a new act in town. It keeps me on my toes, too. It's important to keep adding new things to keep the customers interested." He stroked his chin thoughtfully as he looked at Miki.

Charles took a deep breath. "Maybe . . . you'd like to adopt her!" he said.

Silly Billy looked surprised. "Oh, I wasn't thinking that," he said. "I'd love to have a dog—especially a super-talented dog like this—but my wife is allergic to dogs. No, I was thinking maybe your band and your sweet puppy would like to join me at a performance I'm doing tomorrow, at my nephew's birthday party. He would love Miki." He handed Charles a business card with red, yellow, and blue balloons printed on it. "Why don't you have your parents give me a call?"

# CHAPTER TEN

Lizzie and Charles started bugging Mom and Dad to call Silly Billy right away, and by the time they sat down to dinner that night it was all set. They were going to perform with Silly Billy!

"Your first real gig," Dad said, giving Charles a high five.

"Gig?" Charles asked.

"That's musician talk for a job," Mom explained. Charles gulped. He knew he wasn't a real musician. Silly Billy liked their act, so they must be doing something right. But were they really ready for a "gig"?

"Of course we are," Sammy said, when Charles

called him to share the news. "Well, Miki is, anyway."

Later, Lizzie came into Charles's room and they both plopped down on the bed next to Miki, who had curled up on Charles's pillow. The little white pup lay still, looking more like a stuffie than ever. The dancing must have tired her out. Lizzie stroked her soft fur. "If we keep her much longer, we might have to have her groomed," Lizzie said. "Hypoallergenic dogs like these have hair instead of fur. It just keeps growing longer and longer. We don't want our little Miki to get tangles, do we?"

"Hypoallergenic?" Charles sat straight up when he heard Lizzie say that. "What does that mean, again? Does it mean she makes people sneeze a lot?"

Lizzie shook her head. "No, the opposite. The bichon frise can be a great breed for someone who's allergic."

Charles stared at her. "But that's the only reason Ms. Holly couldn't adopt her. She's allergic!" He remembered the conversation with Silly Billy. "And so is Silly Billy's wife."

"Let's tell Silly Billy that Miki won't make his wife sneeze!" Lizzie jumped up and snatched the card off the bulletin board. "We should call him right now. He'd be the perfect owner for Miki."

Charles grabbed the card out of her hands. "No, I have to ask Ms. Holly first. She loved Miki right away when she saw her. She would be so excited to hear that Miki is hippo—harpy—whatever it is."

Lizzie laughed. "Hypoallergenic," she said. She made it sound easy. "Okay, go ahead and ask Ms. Holly. If she's as nice as you say she is, she'd be a great owner, even if she isn't a performer like Silly Billy."

The next morning Dad drove Charles, Lizzie, and Sammy to the house where the birthday party was taking place. Charles was too busy thinking to really be nervous about their "gig." He was rehearsing what he wanted to tell Ms. Holly. He had left a message on her phone that morning, but she hadn't called back yet. Ms. Holly was going to be so excited when she found out she could adopt Miki after all. As much as Charles hated to give her up, he knew that Miki would be very happy with someone as nice and fun as Ms. Holly.

"Thanks for showing up a little early, kids," said Silly Billy, opening the door when they knocked. "I just wanted to give you an idea of how the show will go. First, we'll do some songs together. Then, I'll probably make some balloon animals, and maybe do a little magic After a while, we'll sing happy birthday and have birthday cake. My wife will bring in the cake she made—she's an amazing baker."

Charles tried to pay attention to what Silly Billy was saying, but he couldn't stop thinking about how exciting it would be when he told Ms. Holly about Miki. He knew that she and Ms. Holly were going to be perfect together.

The performance was going to be in the living room of the house. "I'll introduce you and Miki, and you can jump right into it," he said, showing them how he'd already set up a keyboard and a real drum set. "Just play the way you were playing yesterday, and let Miki dance. I promise, you'll be a big hit."

"I get the drum set!" shouted Sammy.

"No, I do!" said Lizzie.

"You can take turns," said Silly Billy.

They each practiced a drum solo until the party guests began to arrive. Soon it was time for the performance. All the kids—and parents—gathered in the living room. Silly Billy greeted them and introduced the band. "And here are Silly Billy's Willy Nillys!" he said, waving a hand at them, "starring the enchanting Miki!" Charles laughed out loud. Silly Billy had come up with the best band name yet.

There were no balloon animals that day. There was no magic. The only thing the kids wanted was more, more, MORE of Miki's dancing. They loved her. Silly Billy's grin was wider than ever as he watched her dance while Charles, Sammy, and Lizzie banged away on their instruments. Charles couldn't help wondering if Miki's perfect home really was with Silly Billy.

Finally, the kitchen door flew open, and a woman walked in carrying a big birthday cake. "Happy birthday to you," she sang, and even though the cake hid her face Charles knew right away who it was.

It was Ms. Holly.

Wait, what?

Ms. Holly was Silly Billy's wife? Charles stared at her, then at Silly Billy, and saw them smile at each other as she set the cake down in front of the birthday boy. Just as he blew out the candles, Miki must have seen Ms. Holly, too. She dashed through the crowd to greet her, wagging her tail and barking.

*I remember you! I remember all my friends.*

Ms. Holly handed the cake knife to one of the moms and knelt down to sweep the little white pup into her arms. "Miki!" she said.

Silly Billy's eyebrows shot up. "You know Miki?" he asked his wife.

Ms. Holly nodded. "I fell in love with her at first sight, but I didn't tell you about her because I knew you'd say we are too busy to have a dog," she said.

"And I didn't mention her because I know that as much as you want a dog, you're allergic!" said Silly Billy.

"And that's the best part!" cried Charles. Now he could tell Ms. Holly the fantastic news. "That's what I wanted to talk to you about. Miki's coat is hypno—harpo—"

"Hypoallergenic," said Lizzie. "She won't make you sneeze at all."

Ms. Holly stared at them. "Really?" She buried her face in Miki's fur and took a long breath. Then she looked up at her husband. "But we really are very busy," she said. "And I can't have a dog hanging around in a kitchen while I'm teaching people to cook. It's just not professional." She looked very serious.

Silly Billy burst out laughing. "But that's no problem," he said. "If I had a dog like Miki, she would come with me to all my performances. She's a natural star."

"You mean—" Ms. Holly's eyes were wide.

Silly Billy hugged his wife as she held Miki in her arms. "I have a feeling we are all going to be very, very happy together," he said, smiling at Charles.

Charles felt a little twinge in his stomach. Things could not have turned out more perfectly, but it was going to still be so hard to see Miki go. This was always the worst part of being a foster family.

Mom put her arm around Charles and gave him a squeeze. She knew how he was feeling. "I think we've found Miki the best home possible," she whispered to him. "We can feel happy about that."

"Don't forget, you'll get to see her whenever you join me and Miki for a show," said Silly Billy. "And who knows? Maybe we'll all end up on *America's Most Talented Pets* someday."

# PUPPY TIPS

Does your dog have any special talents? Some dogs learn tricks more easily than others, but with patient and kind training, almost any dog can learn to do a few simple tricks that will impress your friends and family. You can find books about teaching dog tricks at your library, or your parents can help you look online. Some good ones to start with are sit pretty, shake hands (or high five), roll over, and take a bow.

Dear Reader,

My dog, Zipper, is more interested in chasing squirrels than learning tricks, but he does know how to sit, shake, and give a high five. He's also very good at rolling over—when he's hoping for a belly rub, that is!

Yours from the Puppy Place,
Ellen Miles

P.S. For other books about dogs who love to perform, try *Sweetie* or *Rusty*.

Lizzie Peterson trudged along the sidewalk, feeling her backpack thump against her shoulders. It was a cloudy gray afternoon in September. The leaves on the trees that lined her street hadn't changed color yet, but you couldn't say they were bright green, either. Their dullness seemed to match her mood.

"What's the matter, Lizzie?" her mom asked when Lizzie arrived home from school.

Lizzie shrugged as she bent down to give her puppy, Buddy, a scritch between the ears. He gazed up at her, his brown eyes shining with happiness, love, and excitement. She couldn't help smiling back at him. Dogs always made her feel better. They had a great attitude, upbeat and ready for anything. At least, Buddy did. He was the best puppy ever, and Lizzie knew how lucky she was that he was part of her family. She reached down to stroke the heart-shaped white patch on Buddy's chest.

"I'm just bored, I guess," she said to her mom. "It's been a while since anything exciting happened."

Mom gave Lizzie a hug, then held her by the shoulders and looked her straight in the eye, smiling. "You mean, since we had a new puppy to foster?" she asked.

Lizzie kicked her sneaker against the floor. Mom always seemed to be able to see straight into her heart. "Maybe," she said. As usual, Mom was right.

The Petersons were a foster family who helped puppies that needed homes. Some puppies had stayed with them for days, while others were there for weeks. Only one, Buddy, had stayed forever. Lizzie's family (her parents; her younger brother, Charles; and their toddler brother, the Bean) had fostered golden retrievers and a Great Dane plus practically every other common breed, as well as mutts large and small. Sometimes Lizzie couldn't believe her good luck. Lizzie had a "Dog Breeds of the World" poster hanging on her bedroom wall, and she loved to draw a red heart next to every breed she'd met or fostered. She'd still never even seen one of those hairless dogs, the Chinese crested, but she was sure she would, one of these days.

"Having a new puppy is always exciting," Mom said. "Don't worry, one always comes along just when you least expect it."

Lizzie gave Buddy one more pat. Then she hung her blue school backpack on a hook by the door and grabbed the green one from the next hook. That was her dog-walking backpack, equipped with a variety of yummy treats, extra leashes and harnesses, and poop bags. "I'd better get going," she said. It was time for work. Lizzie and her best friend Maria (and their two friends, Briana and Daphne) had a very successful dog-walking business, with many happy clients (dogs and people). They were successful because they all loved dogs, and also because they all knew at least a little bit about dog training (Lizzie knew a lot). But the main reason for their success? They were responsible. Lizzie had never once missed a walk, and neither had her friends. They had a perfect record, and all their clients definitely appreciated that.

Lizzie kissed Buddy once more, then stood up tall and stretched. She put on the green backpack. "Okay," she told Mom. "See you later!" She waved as she headed down the front steps.

As she walked, Lizzie thought about other breeds she hadn't met yet. Like a borzoi, a sleek runner with an elegant, swooping chest. Or a big white komondor, a brave protector of sheep with a long, thick coat. She'd never even met a vizsla, or a Norwegian elkhound. But she would. No matter what it took. It was Lizzie's main goal in life to "heart" every dog on her poster.

Lizzie was headed to see her first client, a

young German shepherd named Tank. Tank was big and all muscle, but he was the sweetest, most gentle dog. He wouldn't hurt a fly, even if it landed right on his soft brown nose. Lizzie had brought a pocketful of Tank's favorite treats along (freeze-dried liver), since she planned to work on his leash-walking skills today. She reached in to check that the little brown chunks were there. They were. Good. It was never much use trying to teach dogs if you didn't have excellent treats to offer them.

After Tank, and four other dogs, Lizzie was looking forward to walking her favorite new client: Domino, a peppy little Jack Russell. He was white with black spots, including one near his tail that was the exact shape and size of a domino. He was the happiest dog she'd ever met, and still full of energy even though he was seven years old. Domino was bursting with charm, and being around him never failed to cheer Lizzie up.

The Jacksons, Domino's family, were super sweet. Lizzie knew that when their young twins, Jenny and Merry, got a little older, they would love taking Domino for walks. For now, while the twins were still babies, Mrs. and Mr. Jackson needed help. They adored Domino, but since the kids had come they didn't always have time to give him the exercise he needed.

"Lizzie!" said Mrs. Jackson when she opened the door later that afternoon. "So great to see you. Domino's been off-the-wall excited today, and super hyper." She held a baby in each arm as the little black-and-white pup did figure eights around her feet.

Lizzie dropped to her knees to give Domino a hug. He wriggled in and out of her arms, then spun around in a circle, barking happily. He dashed down the hall, toenails scrabbling, and came prancing back with a giant neon-green alien stuffie. He bit down on it to make it squeak, then tossed it into the air.

*Yay, you're here! Let's play!*

Lizzie laughed. "He always gets this way by Friday," she said. "Then he chills out a little after you hike with him all weekend. He needs adventure in his life."

"Domino does love going on adventures," Mrs. Jackson told Lizzie. "He's been on every high peak in this state and a few others. He's run half marathons, he's ridden down crazy rapids in a red canoe, and he loves to bound through the snow when my husband and I go cross-country skiing."

Mr. and Mrs. Jackson were both tall and lean,

and always seemed to be dressed in sleek black athletic clothes, with special zippers and reflective stripes. The twins went along on all the hikes and runs and ski trails, carried in special sporty backpacks or strapped into fancy strollers.

After she finished walking Domino, Lizzie headed for home. As usual, she was feeling much happier now that she had spent some time with the frisky pup—and all the other dogs.

But she was about to get even happier.

Mom met her at the door. She had a huge smile on her face. "Remember what I said before?" she asked. "About a new foster puppy coming along when you least expect it?"

Lizzie nodded, curious. Her mom grinned as she held up her car keys and gave them a shake so they tinkled like chimes. "Ready to go pick up our new puppy?"

# ABOUT THE AUTHOR

Ellen Miles loves dogs, which is why she has a great time writing the Puppy Place books. And guess what? She loves cats, too! (In fact, her very first pet was a beautiful tortoiseshell cat named Jenny.) That's why she came up with the Kitty Corner series. Ellen lives in Vermont and loves to be outdoors with her dog, Zipper, every day, walking, biking, skiing, or swimming, depending on the season. She also loves to read, cook, explore her beautiful state, play with dogs, and hang out with friends and family.

Visit Ellen at ellenmiles.net.